MW01385759

THE LAZARUS TRIAL

D. DECKKER

DINSU BOOKS

For Subhashini, my love, my anchor, and my greatest support—
your unwavering belief in me fuels every word I write.

And for Sasha, my little light in the darkness—may your curiosity
and imagination always lead you to stories that make the world
feel limitless.

This book is yours, always.

CONTENTS

PREFACE

We were never meant to bring them back.

Science has always been bound by limits—laws of nature, boundaries we were never supposed to cross. But laws can be bent. And boundaries? They can be broken.

At first, it was about **resurrection**.

We thought we were saving lives. That death was just another **medical challenge** to overcome. A problem to be solved.

We were wrong.

Because **death isn't an ending.** It's a **door.**

And every time we opened it, something was **waiting on the other side.**

The Lazarus Trials were supposed to be the future of medicine. The **cure for mortality.**

Instead, they became something else.

Something we **couldn't control.**

Now, the patients who returned are **vanishing.**

Those who remember are **hunted.**

And what came back through the door?

It is awake.

And it is not alone.

Some discoveries should never be made.

Some doors should never be opened.

But it's too late now.

Welcome to The Lazarus Trial.

CHAPTER 1 – THE FIRST REVIVAL

Lazarus Medical Facility – 200 Feet Underground

Dr. Evelyn Carter stepped out of the sterile white elevator into a corridor humming with fluorescent light and the quiet hum of machinery buried deep beneath the earth.

A secret facility. Government-funded. Cut off from the world.

She adjusted her coat, feeling the cool, pressurized air pressing in on her.

This wasn't just any research lab.

This was Project Lazarus.

Ahead, two armed guards stood like statues. Unblinking. Watching her.

Beyond them—the impossible.

A voice cut through the silence. Controlled. Crisp. But too smooth.

"Dr. Carter. Right on time."

She turned.

Dr. Malcolm Thorne approached, his sharp features set in a smile that didn't quite reach his eyes.

Tall. Composed. Too composed.

He offered a handshake. Evelyn hesitated. Took it anyway.

"Dr. Thorne," she said. "I assume you have something extraordinary to show me?"

Thorne smirked. "More than extraordinary."

He turned, leading her down the hall.

"Something... impossible."

The Science Of Resurrection

The observation deck overlooked a surgical chamber lined with reinforced glass.

Inside—a body lay on a hospital gurney.

Male. Late thirties. Unmoving.

Evelyn inhaled sharply. Daniel Reese.

She'd seen his file. Pronounced dead seventeen minutes ago.

Too long.

"You know this won't work," she said.

Thorne didn't react.

"The brain doesn't survive past ten minutes," Evelyn continued. "Even if the heart restarts, neural pathways degrade. Memories collapse. Cells die."

Thorne smiled.

"We've solved that problem."

A nurse handed him a syringe filled with pale-blue liquid.

The Lazarus Serum.

Evelyn narrowed her eyes. "How?"

Thorne twirled the syringe between his fingers.

"We found a way to reactivate neurons before decay begins. By targeting the brainstem and hippocampus, we restart electrical function. Essentially..."

He injected the serum into the IV.

"...we tell the body it never died."

The monitors hummed. The machines waited.

So did Evelyn.

Flatline.

Nothing.

One second. Two.

Still nothing.

Her stomach tightened.

Then—

A single, sharp beep.

She froze.

Another beep.

Then another. Faster. Rhythmic.

The body jerked.

Then Daniel Reese gasped.

The Impossible Becomes Real

His eyes snapped open. Wide. Unfocused.

The air seemed to shift.

Reese's chest heaved. Hands twitched, curling slightly.

"Vitals stabilizing," a nurse whispered. "Brain activity—"

She cut off.

The monitors spiked.

Brain waves shouldn't look like that.

Not after seventeen minutes dead.

Evelyn's fingers curled into her palm.

This was wrong.

And yet—

Reese was alive.

Thorne's Fractured Confidence

Thorne exhaled, tension leaving his shoulders.

Like he'd been holding his breath.

Evelyn caught it.

That moment of doubt.

She narrowed her eyes. "You weren't sure that would work, were you?"

Thorne didn't answer.

It's a second too long.

Then he smiled, but his fingers tapped against his clipboard—just once.

A nervous tic.

Evelyn filed it away.

The First Words

Silence settled.

Reese's breathing slowed.

Then—his lips parted.

His voice wasn't entirely his own.

"Where am I?"

Evelyn took a step forward. "You're safe. You're at the Lazarus Medical Facility."

Reese's eyes twitched. He turned slowly, gaze landing on her.

Then—tears.

It's not normal crying.

Violent. Broken. Uncontrolled.

Evelyn's pulse spiked.

"Daniel?"

His shoulders shook.

And then—a whisper.

"You shouldn't have brought me back."

The Shift In The Room

The air grew colder.

Evelyn didn't move.

"What?"

Reese's breathing quickened. His fingers dug into the sheets.

"No. No, no, no."

Thorne stepped closer. "Daniel, listen to me—"

Reese jerked upright. Eyes darting. Wild. Terrified.

"We weren't supposed to leave."

His heartbeat spiked. Machines screamed warnings.

Nurses rushed in. A guard moved forward.

Evelyn grabbed Reese's wrist. "Daniel, breathe. Tell me what you mean."

His veins pulsed beneath his skin.

His pupils shrank.

Then—his voice changed.

Not his own. Layered. Hollow. Wrong.

"It's watching."

A cold, twisting weight settled in Evelyn's stomach.

Reese's hands curled. He whimpered.

"It's watching me. I can still feel it."

The lights flickered.

Evelyn swore she saw movement.

A shadow that didn't belong.

Then Reese collapsed.

Machines flatlined.

Aftermath

The room was silent.

Daniel Reese lay motionless, chest rising and falling unnaturally slow.

Thorne's jaw tightened.

Evelyn's hands shook.

"What the hell was that?" she demanded.

Thorne didn't answer. Didn't look at her.

CHAPTER 2 – THE LAZARUS EFFECT

Lazarus Medical Facility – Patient Recovery Wing

Daniel Reese wasn't sleeping.

Not in the way he should have been.

It had been three hours since the revival, and his vitals were stable. His body was intact, his heart was beating, and his brain was firing on all cylinders.

Yet—something wasn't right.

Evelyn stood outside his isolation room, watching through the reinforced glass. Inside, Reese sat up in bed, motionless.

Not blinking. Not moving.

Not… human.

"Has he said anything?" she asked.

A nurse beside her, Emily Harlow, shook her head. "Not since he collapsed."

It's watching me. I can still feel it.

The words clung to Evelyn's thoughts.

She exhaled slowly. "Has he slept?"

Emily shifted uncomfortably. "Every time he starts drifting off, he wakes up screaming."

A chill ran down Evelyn's spine.

"Screaming what?"

Emily's voice dropped.

"That something is in the dark. Staring at him."

Reese's Reality Is Breaking

Evelyn stepped inside the room.

Reese didn't react.

Didn't blink. Didn't acknowledge her presence.

His skin looked paler than before, veins pressing blue against the surface.

She pulled up a chair. Sat.

"Daniel," she said carefully.

Still, there was no reaction.

She leaned forward. "Do you know where you are?"

Reese finally turned his head.

Slow. Mechanical.

His pupils were huge, swallowing the hazel of his irises.

"You brought me back."

His voice was distant. Hollow.

Evelyn studied him, keeping her own heartbeat steady.

"Yes," she said. "We did."

Reese blinked just once. "You shouldn't have."

A silence settled between them. Cold. Absolute.

Evelyn cleared her throat. "Daniel, I need to ask you something. Do you know what year it is?"

Stillness.

Then—

"Eighteen twelve."

Evelyn's breath hitched.

"What?" she whispered.

Reese tilted his head. His expression didn't change.

"The war. The cannons were loud. Smoke in the streets. The sea—"

Evelyn's pulse hammered in her throat.

"What war?"

Reese frowned slightly. He looked around like he was seeing the room for the first time.

His hands twitched against the sheets.

"Where is this?"

"This is a medical facility." Evelyn kept her voice even. "You were in an accident. You died. We brought you back."

Reese went very still.

Then he whispered:

"I don't remember dying."

The Screaming In The Dark

Four hours later, alarms blared.

Evelyn bolted toward the sound, racing down the corridor toward Reese's room.

Security shouted orders. A nurse screamed.

She pushed through the door—

And froze.

Reese was on the floor.

Thrashing. Gasping for air.

His hands clawed at his arms, digging deep into his own skin.

"Daniel!" Evelyn rushed forward, grabbing his wrists. "Stop! You're hurting yourself!"

Reese's eyes snapped to hers.

But they weren't his anymore.

They were black.

Deep. Endless. Hollow.

Then—he screamed.

A sound so raw, so full of terror that it sent ice shooting down Evelyn's spine.

His body convulsed, muscles seizing.

She pressed a hand against his chest. "Daniel, breathe. What's happening?"

His lips trembled.

Then—a whisper.

"The dark is not empty."

Evelyn's blood ran cold.

The Symbols

They restrained him. Sedated him.

It didn't stop him.

By the time Evelyn returned to his room, the walls were covered.

Dark, jagged symbols smeared in blood.

His blood.

Reese sat in the corner, legs drawn to his chest, whispering to himself.

Evelyn stared at the symbols—the same ones from the Lazarus files.

She crouched beside him.

"Daniel."

Reese didn't look up.

His fingers still moved against the floor, dragging through his own crimson streaks.

His voice was soft, breathless, almost childlike.

"It's still watching."

The Government Interference

Evelyn barely had time to process what she'd seen before the doors burst open.

Men in black suits stormed the hallway. Their presence was immediate. Heavy. Absolute.

The head of the pack? Agent Rourke.

He walked like someone who didn't waste words. Didn't need to.

The air shifted as he stopped beside her.

"Dr. Thorne," he said, his tone like steel. "You're shutting this down. Now."

Thorne's eyes flared with raw defiance.

"Are you out of your mind? This is history! We've done the impossible!"

Rourke didn't blink. Didn't waver.

"You have no idea what you've done."

Evelyn stepped between them, pulse-pounding.

"Why are you covering this up?"

Rourke's eyes met hers. Unblinking. Cold.

Then he leaned in close.

And whispered—

"Because you don't understand what you brought back."

CHAPTER 3 – A CLOSED CASE

Lazarus Medical Facility – The Final Hours

Dr. Evelyn Carter stared at the manila folder in front of her. CLASSIFIED.

It was heavier than paper should be.

Across from her, Agent Rourke folded his hands on the table. His expression was unreadable.

"You'll sign it," he said.

The non-disclosure agreement lay between them, black ink waiting.

Evelyn didn't move. Didn't even blink.

"This is wrong," she said.

Rourke sighed. Impatient. Cold. "No, Dr. Carter. What's wrong is letting this continue."

Her pulse spiked. "You saw what happened. You heard him. We weren't supposed to bring him back. What does that mean?"

Rourke's jaw tightened.

"You don't want to know."

"I do."

A beat.

Then Rourke leaned forward, his voice lowering.

"Let me be clear. You sign this, walk away, and forget all of it. Or you refuse—"

His eyes locked onto hers.

"And trust me, Dr. Carter, you don't want to see what happens next."

Something in his tone sent ice down her spine.

This wasn't a threat.

It was a promise.

Her fingers hovered over the pen.

This isn't over.

But she signed.

Outside The Facility – The Cold Goodbye

Lazarus's building steel doors slid shut behind her.

Security escorted her out like a disgraced scientist.

No proof. No evidence.

Every trace of what happened to Daniel Reese—gone.

The morning air bit into her skin.

Dr. Malcolm Thorne stood beside her, arms crossed. His expression was unreadable.

"They wiped everything," he muttered.

Evelyn didn't answer.

"Every file. Every record. Like it never happened." His jaw clenched. "We made history. And now it's buried."

Evelyn turned to him.

"Daniel Reese isn't buried."

That shut him up.

Because Reese was still inside.

Still breathing.

Still… something else.

Trying To Forget

Evelyn tried to forget.

Tried to go back to her everyday life.

Tried to convince herself that Lazarus was over.

She lasted three days.

By the fourth, she was digging through medical records she wasn't supposed to have access to.

By the fifth, she had a list of names.

Other Lazarus patients.

And every single one of them was either:

1. Vanished.
2. Dead under strange circumstances.

A Pattern In The Impossible

Evelyn sat in her tiny apartment, files spread across her kitchen table.

Coffee untouched.

Laptop glowing in the dark.

Miriam Wells.

Her name stood out.

Revived five years ago in a private medical study.

Then—erased.

No medical follow-ups. No obituary.

There is no missing person report.

Like she had been wiped from existence.

Evelyn's fingers hovered over the keyboard.

Miriam Wells.

Where the hell are you?

The First Visit – A Dead End?

The address led her to a small town in Pennsylvania.

It was the kind of place where people didn't leave, and strangers weren't welcome.

She knocked on the faded wooden door.

Waited.

Nothing.

Another knock. "Miriam Wells?"

Still nothing.

She was about to leave when the door creaked open.

Just an inch.

A voice. Small. Ragged. Old.

"She's not here."

Evelyn froze.

The voice belonged to a frail woman, deep lines cutting into her face.

Evelyn's gut twisted.

This was her.

Miriam Wells.

She should be forty.

She looked eighty.

Face-To-Face With The Past

Evelyn took a careful step forward.

"I know who you are," she said. "I know what happened to you."

Miriam flinched.

A long, shaky inhale.

Then, softly—

"They said no one would find me."

Evelyn's chest tightened.

Miriam's eyes darted behind Evelyn, scanning the empty road.

Paranoid. Terrified.

"I'm not here to hurt you," Evelyn promised.

Miriam looked at her for a long moment.

Then she whispered, "Did you see them too?"

A chill crept down Evelyn's spine.

"What?"

Miriam's hands trembled.

"The others," she said. "They never leave."

A long, horrible pause.

Miriam's voice dropped lower.

"They stay in the dark."

Her breath hitched.

"And they always watch."

CHAPTER 4 – THE SECOND SURVIVOR

Rural Pennsylvania – A House On The Edge Of Nowhere

Evelyn parked at the end of a long, overgrown driveway. Noah Grant's house loomed ahead.

Small. Rotting at the edges. Windows covered with makeshift wooden planks.

The place reeked of isolation.

She killed the engine. Checked the files in the passenger seat.

Noah Grant. Revived five years ago. No medical records since.

Everyone thought he was dead.

Maybe he should have been.

She stepped out, boots crunching against the gravel. The wind felt wrong. Heavy.

Like something was waiting.

She knocked.

Nothing.

Then—movement. A shadow flickered behind the curtain.

He was watching.

The Paranoia Of The Living Dead

The door cracked open just enough for her to see him.

Noah Grant.

Or what was left of him.

His skin hung loose, pale like wax. Veins visible beneath the surface.

He should have been forty.

He looked sixty.

A single bloodshot eye peered at her through the gap.

"You're not supposed to be here," he whispered.

Evelyn's pulse spiked.

"I need to talk," she said. "It's about Lazarus."

His entire body flinched.

Then the door slammed shut.

The Invitation Inside

She waited.

Footsteps shuffled behind the wood.

Then—the sound of locks being undone.

The door creaked open again.

Noah looked past her, scanning the empty street.

Then he stepped aside—silent permission.

Evelyn walked in.

The inside was worse.

Dark. It smelled of dust, sweat, and something metallic.

The walls were covered in drawings.

Symbols. Circles. Eyes. Jagged lines running together in chaotic spirals.

Evelyn's breath caught.

They were identical to the ones Daniel Reese drew.

Her hands clenched. "You've seen these before."

Noah's voice came flat. Hollow.

"I dream of them."

The Shared Nightmare

Evelyn studied the walls. Every inch is covered.

Some were carved directly into the wood.

"These symbols," she murmured. "Daniel Reese drew the same ones. He's never met you. How is that possible?"

Noah's shoulders were hunched.

He rubbed his arms like he was cold.

"They don't belong to us," he whispered.

Evelyn turned to him. "Then who do they belong to?"

Noah's breath shook.

Then—he laughed.

But it wasn't amusement.

It was fear.

"You really don't get it," he murmured.

Evelyn's stomach tightened.

"Noah, what do they mean?"

He met her eyes.

And then—so softly she barely heard it—

"They never left."

The Truth About 'Them'

Noah ran a shaking hand through his thinning hair.

"I thought it was just me," he muttered. "Thought I was crazy."

Evelyn sat across from him. Waited.

"I hear them when I close my eyes," he whispered. "When the lights go out."

Evelyn's fingers tightened on the table.

"What do you hear?"

Noah's hands twitched.

"Them," he breathed. "Moving. Watching."

Evelyn's pulse pounded.

"What are they?"

Noah shuddered.

"You think we came back alone?" he whispered.

A cold weight settled in Evelyn's chest.

His eyes lifted to hers.

"We weren't alone in the dark."

The Death That Shouldn't Have Happened

Noah grabbed a pen.

Dragged it across a blank scrap of paper.

Another symbol.

Perfectly drawn. Too perfect.

It's like he wasn't guiding his own hand.

Then—his fingers convulsed.

The pen dropped.

His body went rigid.

"Noah?" Evelyn stood.

His eyes rolled back.

His mouth moved, but it wasn't his voice.

Layered. Hollow. Wrong.

"We are awake now. We are awake now."

Evelyn's breath hitched.

"Noah, stay with me." She reached for him—

Then—a violent tremor rocked his body.

His nose bled.

His ears bled.

Then—his eyes.

A single drop of blood slipped down his cheek.

Then another.

Then another.

His body collapsed.

Still. Lifeless.

Evelyn staggered back.

Noah Grant was dead.

The Aftermath

The air in the house felt heavier.

The symbols on the walls seemed darker.

Evelyn's hands shook.

This wasn't a coincidence.

Daniel. Noah. Miriam.

Every single one of them left Lazarus different.

And now—

They were dying.

One by one.

And something was watching.

CHAPTER 5 – PROJECT LAZARUS

The cursor blinked.

Final key sequence entered.

A brief pause—then the system shell cracked open.

Access granted.

Evelyn exhaled sharply.

She'd done it.

The Lazarus archives were buried behind layers of quantum-encrypted firewalls, air-gapped redundancies, and biometric access keys.

It had taken three backdoors, a deepfake access token, and a virtual proxy chain bouncing through five continents.

Even then, it should've been impossible.

But now—

She was in.

Hundreds of classified files. Research logs. Human trials.

Her fingers hovered over the keyboard.

A single document stood out.

LAZARUS TRIALS – HUMAN MIND TRANSFER PROGRAM

Evelyn's stomach tightened.

She clicked.

And the truth unraveled.

Lazarus Was Never About Resurrection

Text scrolled across the screen. Official government headers. Top-tier clearance levels.

PROJECT LAZARUS PRIMARY OBJECTIVE:
To develop a sustainable process for neural pattern migration into biologically viable hosts.

Evelyn's pulse spiked.

She clicked deeper into the file, bypassing the automated security sweeps using an AI-scrambled identity key.

More reports.

More hidden subroutines.

They Weren't Reviving The Dead. They Were Extracting Minds.

She scanned the logs.

Subject 04: The initial transfer attempt resulted in residual neural noise—indicating the presence of foreign cognitive artifacts.

Foreign cognitive artifacts.

Residual neural noise.

She felt a cold sweat forming.

Lazarus wasn't just reviving people.

They were trying to upload minds.

The ultra-rich. The powerful. They weren't trying to cheat death through medicine.

They wanted new bodies.

But something had gone wrong.

The Failed Transfers

She scrolled faster, bypassing black-barred redactions using a software exploit running in the background.

Test Log 26-7A

SUBJECT 04: "I can hear them."

DOCTOR: "Your vitals are stable. Do you know your name?"

SUBJECT 04: *"No. No, no, no, no—this isn't—"*

DOCTOR: "Breathe. Your memory will return shortly."

SUBJECT 04: "There's something inside. I can feel it."

Evelyn's breath hitched.

She scanned further.

Test Log 39-8F

SUBJECT 12: "I was somewhere else."

DOCTOR: "That's a common neurological response. The migration protocol—"

SUBJECT 12: "No. No. No. This body was empty. But I wasn't the first inside."

DOCTOR: "Explain."

SUBJECT 12: (whispering) *"We weren't alone in the dark."*

Evelyn's fingers clenched into fists.

They had assumed the bodies were empty.

That the original neural maps had been erased.

But they weren't.

Or worse—something else had moved in.

Her vision blurred as she scrolled to the final test entry.

Test Log 42-9X (CLASSIFIED - REDACTED)

The entire file was blacked out.

No timestamps.

No identifiers.

Just one line left visible.

"The experiment is complete. The door is open."

The Call That Shouldn't Have Come

Her laptop beeped.

She jerked back.

Incoming call. Unknown number.

Evelyn's pulse spiked.

She let it ring.

Then—she answered.

Silence.

Then, a voice she hadn't heard since Lazarus was shut down.

Dr. Malcolm Thorne.

"You need to listen to me," he said.

His voice shook.

Evelyn's grip tightened.

"Where the hell are you?"

"It doesn't matter," he rasped. "What matters is what you found."

Her laptop glowed in the dark. The words **HUMAN MIND TRANSFER PROGRAM** are still on-screen.

"You knew," she said.

A long pause.

Then—a bitter, humorless laugh.

"I didn't know everything."

Evelyn's stomach knotted. "What went wrong, Thorne?"

His breath shuddered through the line.

"You don't understand," he whispered.

"The human body is just a host. A machine."

Her fingers tightened.

Thorne exhaled.

"Sometimes," he continued, voice cracking, "when you move

someone out—"

A pause.

"—something else moves in."

"What is that something?" she asked.

But the line went dead.

The Entity's Influence

Evelyn's skin went cold.

Her laptop screen flickered.

The Lazarus file glitched.

Then—erased itself.

Letter by letter, the words vanished.

Her heart slammed against her ribs.

She yanked the power cord.

Too late.

The screen went black.

Then—

A whisper.

Soft. Right behind her ear.

"We are awake now."

Evelyn spun.

Nothing there.

But the air felt wrong.

Like something had been watching.

And now—it knew her.

CHAPTER 6 – THE HIVE MIND

Evelyn's Apartment – 3:14 Am

The cursor blinked.

Her code was executed flawlessly.

A secure tunnel opened to Lazarus's offsite backup storage.

She wasn't supposed to have access. But she did.

Lazarus had revoked her credentials and wiped her from the system.

But she'd left herself a backdoor before they locked her out.

One that bypassed internal security redundancies and routed through an external vendor's cloud backup.

She had sixty seconds max.

She launched the query.

TARGET: Surveillance Backup Logs – Lazarus Isolation Wing
TIME FRAME: Last 24 Hours
ACCESS LEVEL: System Administrator

The server responded.

Access Granted.

Her pulse spiked.

She selected Room 314 – Daniel Reese.

The footage loaded.

Her fingers hovered over the keyboard.

She played the footage back—frame by frame.

Daniel Reese's Impossible Escape

12:02 AM – Reese is still in bed. Unmoving.

12:03 AM – The camera feed flickered—a ripple, like digital interference.

Evelyn leaned in.

12:03:22 AM – Something shifted.

Not Reese.

The shadows in the corner of the room.

They moved.

Like they had weight.

Like they were watching.

Evelyn's breath hitched.

12:03:45 AM – The screen glitched harder.

Static rolled over the feed.

And then—

Reese sat up.

Not normal.

Too fast.

A sharp, unnatural jerk.

Like a puppet being yanked by invisible strings.

Evelyn's pulse thundered.

12:04 AM – The screen ripped into static.

A single frame flashed.

A face.

Not Reese's.

Not human.

Just—black eyes. Empty. Endless.

And then—darkness.

Evelyn jerked back.

The file was gone.

Deleted.

She Wasn't Alone in the System

Her laptop pinged.

UNAUTHORIZED ACCESS DETECTED.

Shit.

She'd triggered an internal security flag.

A new window popped up.

INCOMING CALL – UNKNOWN NUMBER

Her stomach knotted.

She let it ring.

Then—she answered.

A voice she knew.

Dr. Raymond Ellis.

"Jesus Christ, Carter—what the hell did you just do?"

Ellis Knows She's Inside

Evelyn closed her eyes.

"Ellis. I need more time."

"You just pinged an unauthorized admin login from an offsite location. You think I'm the only one who noticed?"

She swallowed.

"Did anyone else—?"

"Not yet. But if they run a second sweep, you're screwed."

She exhaled. She tried to steady herself.

"I need access to Lazarus. Now."

Ellis cursed under his breath.

"You're insane."

"You don't understand," she pressed. "Daniel Reese didn't escape. He was taken. And I think the other Lazarus patients are—"

A sharp beep cut her off.

Her screen went black.

Then—

The cursor moved.

On its own.

A single line typed itself.

"We are awake now."

Her laptop shut down.

And the lights in her apartment flickered.

Evelyn's breath came ragged.

Ellis's voice dropped.

"Carter. What did you see?"

She licked her lips.

"You wouldn't believe me."

A pause.

Then—Ellis sighed.

"Meet me at the north entrance in twenty minutes."

The call ended.

Evelyn grabbed her keys.

She wasn't just hacking Lazarus anymore.

She was going back inside.

Back Inside Lazarus

Twenty-two minutes later, she stepped through the emergency

entrance.

The system read Ellis's ID badge.

Green light. Access granted.

No alarms. No questions.

She was a ghost in a building that had already tried to erase her.

The Linked Patients

She moved fast.

Straight to Data Archives.

By sunrise, she was knee-deep in confidential reports.

And that's when she found it.

A classified Lazarus file buried deep in the system.

MULTIPLE REVIVED PATIENTS DISPLAY SYNCHRONIZED BEHAVIOR.

Her breath hitched.

Evelyn clicked.

Lines of case notes filled the screen.

"Subjects exhibit coordinated speech patterns despite no prior contact."

"Patients across different locations display identical motor responses in real-time."

"Electroencephalography scans indicate synchronized neural activity between subjects miles apart."

Her hands tightened on the keyboard.

This wasn't a coincidence.

This was something else.

A hive mind.

A Name That Shouldn't Be There

She kept reading.

A list of patients linked to the phenomenon.

Then—her heart stopped.

Daniel Reese.

Listed among them.

Before he ever escaped.

She inhaled sharply.

The connection existed before he left.

Before he even woke up.

This wasn't them communicating.

This was them being controlled.

The Abandoned Hospital

The address came from a police report.

An old psychiatric facility. Abandoned.

Someone had broken in the night before.

A single message had been left on the walls.

Written in something dark. Wet.

Evelyn pulled up the attached crime scene photo.

Her stomach turned.

A single phrase sprawled across the decaying walls.

"The door is open."

Her breath hitched.

She had seen those words before.

In Noah Grant's house.

In Daniel Reese's file.

And now—here.

Something Is Coming

Evelyn parked outside the hospital, staring at the crumbling structure.

The air felt different here.

Heavy.

Like the world was holding its breath.

She pushed open the rusted doors, flashlight in hand.

Darkness stretched endlessly ahead.

The halls smelled of decay and time.

She moved carefully, footsteps echoing.

Then—she saw it.

The words.

"The door is open."

Scrawled in something thick and black.

Her fingers trembled.

Then—

A sound.

A whisper.

But not one voice.

Many.

Layered. Twisting.

"We are awake now."

The flashlight flickered.

The air shuddered.

Evelyn's breath hitched.

She wasn't alone.

And whatever had been watching through Daniel Reese—

Was finally awake.

CHAPTER 7 –
THE RETURN OF
DR. THORNE

Evelyn's Apartment – 10:13 Pm

The email arrived without a sender.

No subject. Nobody.

It's just an attachment.

Evelyn's stomach tightened as she clicked.

The image loaded.

A security camera still.

From inside her own apartment.

Her breath hitched.

The timestamp: 30 minutes ago.

She scanned the dimly lit photo.

Nothing looked out of place. Nothing was there.

But she was alone.

Wasn't she?

Her phone buzzed.

UNKNOWN CALLER.

She hesitated. Then answered.

Silence.

Then—a whisper.

"We are waiting."

The line cut.

Evelyn's breath came shaky, uneven.

She checked the email again.

Below the image are the coordinates.

A motel.

Middle of nowhere.

She grabbed her jacket and keys.

She had no choice.

She had to go.

An Isolated Motel – 11:48 Pm

Evelyn pulled up to the run-down motel, the only car in the lot parked outside Room 206.

The light was on.

She killed the engine.

Her hands tightened on the steering wheel.

This was it.

She stepped out, boots crunching against the gravel.

The door to 206 was slightly open.

A whisper of movement inside.

She knocked. Once.

Silence.

Then—a voice she hadn't heard since Lazarus shut down.

"Come in."

She pushed the door open.

Dr. Malcolm Thorne stood in the dim light.

Thorne's Hiding Place

The room was a disaster.

Stacks of papers. Medical files. Scribbled notes pinned to the walls.

A half-packed duffel bag sat by the bed.

Thorne himself looked like a ghost.

Unshaven. Eyes red-rimmed.

Like a man who hadn't slept in days.

Evelyn folded her arms. "You've been running."

Thorne let out a dry, humorless laugh.

"Wouldn't you?"

She scanned the mess around him. "Why now? Why call me?"

He met her eyes.

"Because you won't stop."

A pause.

"Because you need to understand what you're chasing."

The Ultimate Truth

Thorne exhaled. Ran a hand through his graying hair.

Then—softly, carefully—

"We weren't bringing people back."

Evelyn's stomach tightened.

Thorne's gaze darkened.

"We were letting something in."

A chill raced down her spine.

She swallowed hard. "What does that mean?"

Thorne sat on the edge of the bed.

Shaking his head.

"We thought we were reviving them. Thought we were saving lives."

A bitter chuckle.

"But every time we pulled one back..."

His hands clenched.

"The barrier got thinner."

Death Is A Door

Evelyn sat across from him. Leaning in.

"You said death is a door," she pressed. "Explain it."

Thorne exhaled.

"It's not some poetic metaphor."

His fingers tapped against the table.

"Think about it. You die. Your brain stops. But what if consciousness—true consciousness—doesn't just 'end'?"

He rubbed his face—a slow, shuddering breath.

"What if it lingers? Stays just beyond reach?"

Evelyn's pulse quickened.

"We assumed we were just reactivating neurons. Rebooting the system."

His eyes met hers.

"But what if something else had already taken residence?"

Her breath caught.

The Missing Patients Never Came Back

Evelyn's voice was barely a whisper.

"The missing patients."

Thorne nodded.

"They didn't disappear."

He swallowed hard.

"They never came back."

Evelyn's hands tightened on her lap.

"What are they now?"

A long silence.

Then—Thorne's voice, barely audible.

"Not human anymore."

What's On The Other Side?

Evelyn pressed her palms to her temples.

Tried to think.

"Okay. If the body dies and the mind is wiped... what takes its place?"

Thorne's jaw tightened.

"We don't know."

He exhaled, frustrated.

"We assumed they were brain-dead until reactivation. But the truth is... whatever comes back?"

He looked away.

"It already knows things it shouldn't."

Evelyn felt a slow, creeping dread.

Daniel Reese.

Noah Grant.

The symbols.

The whispers.

The multi-voice echoes.

Something had been waiting.

And now?

It was here.

The Knock At The Door

A sharp knock.

Evelyn and Thorne froze.

Her pulse spiked.

Thorne's face went white.

Three knocks.

Measured. Slow.

Evelyn's stomach twisted.

Then—a voice from the other side of the door.

"Dr. Carter."

She knew that voice.

Her breath caught.

Daniel Reese.

CHAPTER 8 – THE LAST STAND

Motel Room – 12:13 Am

The knock still echoed.

Daniel Reese was outside.

Evelyn's pulse thundered.

Thorne shook his head. Mouth dry. "We can't open it."

Another knock.

Three slow raps. Precise. Measured.

Then—the handle turned.

The door swung open.

And Daniel Reese stepped inside.

Daniel Reese Is Not Daniel Reese

His skin was pale, stretched too tight over his bones.

His eyes—black. Hollow. Endless.

But his lips curled into a familiar smile.

"Dr. Carter," he greeted like nothing had happened.

Evelyn couldn't move.

Couldn't breathe.

"Daniel?"

His head tilted. Just slightly. Too precise.

"You look surprised."

Thorne's breath hitched.

"You're not him," he whispered.

Reese's smile widened.

"Not entirely."

The Government Steps In

Before Evelyn could respond—tires screeched outside.

The roar of engines.

Then—a crash.

Evelyn ran to the window.

Black SUVs. Government plates.

Doors burst open.

Men in suits. Armed. Coming straight for them.

Thorne swore. "It's Rourke."

Evelyn turned back to Reese.

He hadn't moved.

Didn't even react.

He just... watched.

"They're too late," he whispered.

Face-To-Face With Rourke

The door slammed open.

Agent Rourke strode in, gun drawn.

His face—tight, unreadable.

"Step away from him."

Evelyn's hands clenched.

"Rourke, what the hell is this?"

He ignored her.

Eyes locked on Reese.

"You're coming with us."

Reese laughed.

Low. Cold. Wrong.

"Are you sure?"

Rourke didn't waver.

"Get on the ground. Now."

Reese's smile didn't fade.

But he lifted his hands. Slowly.

"Your call," he said.

Then—Rourke's phone rang.

A number with no name.

His expression shifted.

He hesitated.

Then—answered.

The Call That Changes Everything

Evelyn watched as Rourke's face drained of color.

His grip on the gun tightened.

Then—he lowered it.

Eyes flicked to Reese.

Then, back to Evelyn.

"You need to come with us," he said. It's not a demand. Its a warning.

Evelyn stepped forward.

"What did they say?"

Rourke didn't answer.

Didn't have to.

Because behind him—the lights flickered.

The air shifted.

And Reese… began to laugh.

When we looked back, he was not there anymore.

The Gathering Of The Lazarus Patients

They arrived at the abandoned airstrip just before dawn.

Evelyn barely processed it.

The number of people.

Dozens. Hundreds.

All were standing together.

Faces blank. Eyes black.

Moving in perfect unison.

Daniel Reese led them.

Their voices rose as one.

Chanting.

An ancient, guttural language.

Words that felt wrong.

Thorne's breath shook.

"What the hell is this?"

Evelyn's pulse pounded.

And then she saw it.

A mark on the ground.

Drawn in ash and blood.

A circle. A gateway.

And the chanting grew louder.

The Ritual

Evelyn grabbed Rourke's arm.
"What are they doing?"
Rourke's jaw tightened.
"They're opening the door."
Thorne swore.
The wind picked up.
A hum filled the air.
The circle began to glow.
And Daniel Reese smiled.
Then—
The ground cracked open.

CHAPTER 9 – THE CHOICE

The Ritual Worked.

Evelyn couldn't breathe.

The ground split open at the center of the Lazarus circle.

A void. A space that shouldn't exist.

Blackness spilled out, creeping like smoke.

The wind whipped around them—but the patients didn't move.

Hundreds of them. Still. Unblinking.

Daniel Reese stood at the center.

Smiling.

The Other Side Is Awake

Evelyn felt it before she saw it.

A pull.

Like the space beyond the door wanted her to step forward.

Her ears rang. Her vision blurred.

Then—a voice.

Layered. Hollow. Deep.

"You have seen the door."

Evelyn staggered.

"Now you must choose."

Her heart slammed against her ribs.

And then—she knew.

The Lazarus research wasn't just opening a door.

It was an invitation.

And something on the other side had been waiting.

Rourke's Final Warning

A hand grabbed her arm.

Rourke.

Face pale. Eyes wide with fear.

"We have to stop this."

His gun was raised. But Evelyn knew—it wouldn't matter.

This wasn't something you shot.

Thorne's voice was raw, panicked. "We have to burn it all. Every file. Every record."

Evelyn's mind raced.

Destroy it?

Or use it?

One would close the door. Forever.

The other—

Would show her the truth.

Evelyn's Choice

She stepped closer to the cracked earth.

Thorne grabbed her wrist.

"Don't do this."

Her pulse pounded.

She looked at the Lazarus patients—linked, controlled, changed.

Daniel Reese watching her.

Smiling.

Waiting.

Her voice came quiet.

"What's on the other side?"

Reese's blackened eyes reflected nothing.

But his smile widened.

And then, he whispered:

"Come and see."

She Steps Forward

The research could be destroyed.

She could walk away.

But…

Then what?

She would never know.

Never understand.

Her whole life had been about answers.

And now—the final one was in front of her.

She stepped closer.

Rourke swore. "Evelyn—"

Thorne lunged—too late.

Evelyn fell forward.

Into the dark.

The Last Patient Disappears

The ground sealed behind her.

The wind died.
The chanting stopped.
And Daniel Reese?
He was gone.
The patients blinked once.
And then—one by one—
They collapsed.
The night went silent.
And on the cold, cracked pavement—
A final message.
Scrawled in blood.
"We are awake now."

EPILOGUE – THE OTHER SIDE

There was no air.

No light.

No ground beneath her feet.

Evelyn wasn't falling.

She wasn't floating, either.

She just was.

A space that shouldn't exist.

A space that had been waiting.

Then—

The whisper.

"You wanted to see."

The Landscape Of The Dead

Shapes began to form.

Not buildings. Not land.

Memories.

Flickering images. A battlefield. Smoke. Blood. A man screaming in a language she didn't know.

A hospital. Machines humming. A woman gasping for air.

A child in the dark, whispering "I don't want to go."

Evelyn's breath caught.

This place was made of them.
The ones who had died.
And the ones who hadn't come back alone.
She turned. And saw them.

The Others

Figures.
Tall. Impossible.
Not men. Not bodies.
Shadows, shifting in and out of form.
Eyes too many.
Mouths that didn't move, but still spoke.
"You opened the door."
Their voices weren't loud.
But they filled everything.
"Now we do not have to wait."
Evelyn staggered back.
"Wait for what?" she whispered.
One of the figures tilted its head.
"For you."

The Meaning Of Lazarus

Images flashed through her mind.
Daniel Reese. Black eyes. A voice not his own.
The Lazarus patients standing in perfect unison.
Thorne whispering, "We weren't bringing people back."
It wasn't a mistake.

It had never been a mistake.

The Lazarus project had never been about saving lives.

It was about letting something in.

A way for them to return.

Her stomach dropped.

"You used us."

The figures didn't move.

Didn't deny it.

They didn't need to.

Because she knew.

She had always known.

What Happens Next?

The space began to crack.

Not break.

Open.

A way through.

A way out.

A way in.

The figures stepped forward.

Evelyn felt the pull.

She had one chance.

To stop it.

To close the door.

Or—

To become something else.

Her lips parted.

She made her choice.

And then—
Evelyn Carter disappeared.

The World Remembers Too Late

The Lazarus files were erased.

Thorne vanished.

Rourke never spoke of it again.

The patients who had been revived?

Their bodies were found empty.

And on the walls of the abandoned hospital—

A final message.

One no one could explain.

Scrawled in something not human.

"SHE IS AWAKE NOW."

AFTERWORD

There are stories about life after death—about tunnels of light, about voices calling from beyond. About souls drifting between worlds.

But what if we got it wrong?

What if death isn't a passage but a **barrier**?

What if consciousness doesn't simply **fade** but lingers, waiting for something to take its place?

The **Lazarus Trials** began as a scientific revolution, a bold attempt to **rewrite the limits of human existence**. But in the end, they didn't just change medicine.

They changed **everything.**

We sought to pull people back from the grave, but we never stopped to ask:

What if something else was trying to come through?

The truth is, we still don't understand what we awakened. The patients who returned—the ones who still walk among us—are not the same.

Maybe they never were.

Maybe **the ones we lost never came back at all.**

And if that's true…

Then death isn't just the **end of life.**

It's the **beginning of something else.**

Something we were never supposed to see.

Something that **is still watching.**

And if you're reading this—**it already knows your name.**

ACKNOWLEDGEMENT

Writing *The Lazarus Trial* was a journey into the unknown—a deep dive into the intersection of science, horror, and the fragile line between life and death. But no journey is ever taken alone.

First and foremost, I want to thank My Wife, whose unwavering support, late-night conversations, and constant encouragement kept this story alive even when the shadows of doubt crept in.

To my **friends and family**, who tolerated my obsession with medical mysteries, experimental science, and the terrifying possibilities of resurrection—you made this book possible simply by believing in it.

To the **readers**, the ones who crave stories that push the boundaries of what we understand, who are willing to stare into the abyss and wonder *what if*—this book is for you.

To the **scientists, doctors, and researchers** who dedicate their lives to understanding the complexities of the human brain, the boundaries of consciousness, and the nature of death—your work is the foundation of both horror and hope.

And finally, to **those who have ever questioned what happens after we die**—perhaps the truth is something far stranger than we ever imagined.

Some doors should never be opened. But thank you for walking through this one with me.

ABOUT THE AUTHOR

D. Deckker

Dinesh Deckker is a multifaceted author and educator with a distinguished academic and professional background, holding a BSc Hons in Computer Science, a BA (Hons), and an MBA from prestigious UK institutions, and currently pursuing a PhD in Marketing. With a career dedicated to blending technology, education, and literature, Dinesh has further honed his craft through specialized courses from globally renowned  institutions, including programs in creative writing, early childhood education, psychology, and journalism from universities such as UC Santa Cruz, Yale, Wesleyan, and Johns Hopkins. His extensive qualifications encompass diverse areas like literacy acquisition, writing for young readers, poetry workshops, and teaching writing, equipping him with a comprehensive understanding of storytelling, educational methods, and creative expression. Dinesh's passion for lifelong learning and his dedication to the craft of writing are evident in his works, which seamlessly integrate his expertise in education, technology, and literature, making him a versatile and engaging voice in his field.

BOOKS BY THIS AUTHOR

Last Forest: A Climate Change Dystopia And Eco-Fiction Novel

In a world where forests are extinct and oxygen is a commodity controlled by Genesis Corp, humanity survives under domed cities, breathing only what they can afford. But when scientist Liana Vos uncovers a buried truth—evidence that the Earth was healing long before Genesis silenced it—she becomes the most wanted fugitive on the planet.

A Killer Among Them: Dark Psychological Detective Fiction

Detective Elias Monroe is hunting a brutal serial killer terrorizing the city—leaving behind cryptic Latin messages and a trail of gruesome crime scenes. Each victim is tied to past injustices, each murder a carefully orchestrated act of vengeance.

As evidence mounts, Elias spirals into a desperate race against time—fighting to piece together the truth before the next victim falls. But the deeper he digs, the more he realizes that the real danger isn't just the murders—it's his own mind.

Suicide: A Psychological Thriller

Alex stood at the edge of a towering mountain, believing there was no way forward—until fate intervened. A single misstep sends him plummeting, not into death, but into a brutal fight for survival. Trapped 1,000 meters above the ground, hanging onto a fragile branch, Alex is faced with a terrifying truth: He must choose between surrendering to despair or battling his way back to life.

Shadows Of Fallout

In the aftermath of a catastrophic event, the world lies in ruins, and humanity faces its greatest challenge yet: survival. Among the chaos, a group of unlikely companions must navigate a desolate landscape, confronting danger, loss, and their own inner battles.